THE EVENT

DANIEL GRANT

PART 6

THIS IS A WORK OF FICTION.

NAMES, CHARACTERS, BUSINESSES, PLACES, EVENTS AND INCIDENTS ARE EITHER THE PRODUCTS OF THE AUTHOR'S IMAGINATION OR USED IN A FICTITIOUS MANNER. ANY RESEMBLANCE TO ACTUAL PERSONS, LIVING OR DEAD, OR ACTUAL EVENTS IS PURELY COINCIDENTAL.

NO ONE UNDER THE AGE OF CONSENT, IN WHATEVER JURISDICTION YOU HAPPEN TO FIND YOURSELF, SHOULD EVEN CONSIDER READING THIS COMIC. IF YOU DO, IT'S VERY LIKELY TO PERMANANTLY SHRIVEL YOUR SEX ORGANS.

YOU'VE BEEN WARNED.

THIS COMIC CONTAINS ALL THE GOOD STUFF, NUDITY, SEX AND VIOLENCE. IF ANY OF THE ABOVE CAUSE YOU ANGST --

PLEASE DO NOT READ ANY FURTHER.

ISBN-13: 978-1-948297-21-9

DALLENT

OUR INVITE? DAMN WE MUST HAVE LEFT IT AT HOME!
THAT IS ONE FREAKY LOOKING HAT, MISTER.
WELL, THAT'S ONE FREAKY LOOKING BALD HEAD, YOUNG MAN.
NO NEED TO INSULT, SIR.
MALCOLM, MAYBE WE SHOULDN'T GET IN A PISSING CONTEST WITH THE MAN WHEN WE'RE STILL TRYING TO FIND DARCI!
RIGHT!
DARCI, YOU SAY?

YES! DO YOU KNOW HER?
HAVE YOU SEEN HER?
LET'S SEE. SUPER HOT CHICK, GREAT TITS, ASS YOU COULD BOUNCE A QUARTER OFF OF.
I'M NOT HEARING THIS!
GRRR!
KEEP IT TOGETHER, MIKE. EYE ON THE BRASS RING.
RIGHT!
THAT SOULNDS LIKE IT COULD BE HER.
POTENTIALLY, COULD BE HER.
NOT THAT I'VE EVER CHECKED HER OUT IN THAT WAY!

WELL, I'VE JUST DESCRIBED EVERY DAMN WOMAN IN THIS PLACE, GENTLEMEN.
WHAT ARE YOU REALLY UP TO? DECIDED TO COME UP TO GREAT WHITE NORTH, BAG YOUR LIMIT OF PUSSY AND THEN HEAD BACK TO THE STATES.
I CAN ASSURE YOU THAT WAS NEVER OUR INTENTION.
UNLESS THAT'S A POSSIBILITY?
I'M HAVING A BIT OF A SEXUAL DRY SPELL.
MALCOLM!
JUST ASKING, MIKE!
I MET A WOMAN RECENTLY THAT SORT OF CHANGED MY SEXUAL MINDSET.
SO --
OF LATE, I REALIZED I'M LOOKING FOR THE KIND OF WOMAN WHO MIGHT TAKE ME UNDER HER WING, SO TO SPEAK.
AND --
I'VE ALSO REALIZED I'M RATHER TURNED ON BY ASIAN WOMEN.

GRRR!
MALCOLM, YOU'RE OVERSHARING AGAIN!
ASIAN AND SHALL WE SAY NURTURING IN A DEMANDING SORT OF WAY.
DO YOU KNOW ANY LADIES AROUHND HERE THAT MIGHT FIT THE BILL?
DO I LOOK LIKE A DATING SERVICE TO YOU, BONEHEAD?
I JUST THOUGHT IF IF YOU DID KNOW SOMEONE --
I AM SO GOING TO SHOOT THESE ASSHOLES AND DUMP THEIR BODIES IN THE DRINK!

WE SHOULD SHAVE YOUR HEAD BEFORE WE HANG YOU!
UP ON HER TOES, THAT'S GOTTA SUCK.
DOESN'T HANGING SEEM A BIT HARSH, GUYS.
WE COULD SIMPLY EXILE HER TO ELFLAND. SHE'LL SUFFER PLENTY THERE.
SHE'S RENDERED US USELESS AS MEN!
DON'T YOU MEAN MORE USELESS, OLIVER!
YOU WHEENIE!

THE HELL WITH EXILE. I SAY HANG THE BITCH!
THE SUBMISSIVE CUNT HAS DONE A DAMN GOOD JOB OF HIDING THE GATEWAYS!
WITHOUT CONTROL OF THE PORTALS, MY ENTIRE COUP GOES DOWN IN FLAMES!
NOW I'LL BE FORCED TO WASTE TIME TORTURING THE LOCATIONS OUT OF THAT WOULD-BE MISTRESS, WHICH COULD BE REALLY FUN, BUT I JUST WANTED TO TAKE CONTROL WITHOUT FUSS AND START REMAKING THIS DOMAIN IN MY OWN EVIL IMAGE.
THE DECISION TO HANG HER WAS A BIT HASTY -- AS WAS THE COUP. I GOT RATHER CARRIED AWAY BY THE OCCASION.
AND --
IF I DON'T, I'LL APPEAR WEAK TO MY NEWLY ACQUIRED SLAVES.
IF I DO HANG HER, THERE WILL BE REPRISALS FROM THOSE CHARTER BITCHES.

THE ROLEPLAYING AT THIS EVENT IS SO INVOLVED.
I CAN'T BELIEVE I'VE IMMEDIATELY FOUND THE UPPER ECHELON OF SEX CLUBS.
I WONDER WHAT IT WOULD BE LIKE TO BE THE QUEEN OF MY OWN DOMAIN.
DR. FAIRCHILD REALLY DID ME A SOLID HOOKING ME UP WITH THESE CHARTER FOLKS.
WHO ARE YOU KIDDING DARCI, YOU'D FOLD FASTER THAN THE MISTRESS DID.
OH, BLESSED SUBMISSION!
DAMN GATORS!
HUH?
HUH?
HUH?
HUH?

ROAR
AHHHH

YOU GUYS HEAR THAT?
AHHHHH
ROAR
THAT IS THE SWEET SOUND OF OLD FRED FLUSHING OUT A FLAG FOR US.
BE READY, AND REMEMBER DARCI IS OUR CAPTURE.
FIRST TIME OUT THEY ALWAYS RUN TOGETHER.
SO --
WE'VE GOT TO KEEP BRENDA PROTECTED.
DON'T WORRY, LT, WE'LL GET HER.
DAMN RIGHT WE WILL TROOPS.
GET READY!
SOMEONE PLEASE HELP US!

AHHHHH
GATOR!
ROAR
FUCKING GATOR, GUYS!
RUMBLE
RUMBLE
BACK OFF FRED!

ALLIGATORS JUST AREN'T SEXY!
EARTH TO BEAUTIFUL!
HUH?
I'M GLAD MY PROPOSED SOMEWHAT IMMINENT DEMISE AMUSES YOU DARCI!
SO, EVIL!
I REALLY WISH YOU'D STOP SAYING THAT, CODY!
IT'S NOT THAT --
NOW, WAIT JUST A MINUTE, SISTER, YOU'RE THE ONE WHO VOLUNTARILY PUT HER FOOL NECK IN THE NOOSE.

I'M A NATURAL BORN SUBMISSIVE, DARCI!
IT'S NEARLY IMPOSSIBLE FOR ME TO SAY 'NO'!
WELL, YOU MUST HAVE BEEN A FUN DATE IN HIGH SCHOOL!
INSULTS AT A TIME LIKE THIS, DARCI?
THE ROLEPLAYING JUST NEVER ENDS WITH THESE FOLKS?
SOMETIMES, I WISH THEY'D BREAK CHARACTER AND JUST GIVE SOME FURTHER EXPLANATION OF THE STORY LINE.

Risk

AREN'T WE SUPPOSED TO BE LOOKING FOR A GATEWAY THAT WILL SEND US ON TO THE BIG SEX PARTY AT THE FINAL DOMAIN?
THE GATEWAY --
Risk
FUNNY YOU SHOULD MENTION IT.
DON'T MAKE ME TORTURE THE LOCATION OUT OF YOU SLUT!
TORTURE?
I'M A SUB.
I THRIVE ON TONTURE, MISTRESS!
THIS WON'T BE VIBRATOR TO PUSSY TORTURE SLUT. YOU WILL EXPERIENCE REAL AGONY!
Risk Pool

OBVIOUSLY, I'M LESS KEEN ON THAT SORT OF TORTURE, MISTRESS.
MISTRESS, SOME OF US HAVE BEEN TALKING.
IS THAT SO?
YES, MISTRESS --
SOME OF US FEEL, NOT ME OF COURSE.
THAT TORTURE AND DEATH IS A LITTLE OVER THE TOP.
OH!

I DON'T THINK SHE WAS THE WORST MISTRESS IN THE WORLD.
MORE INEPTITUDE WITHIN THE ROLE THAN HAVING EVIL INTENT.
OH, I SEE WHERE THIS IS LEADING.
A SLAVE REVOLT ON TOP OF A SLAVE REVOLT.
HOW FUN!
SLAVE REVOLT?
WE AT THE GUILD KNOW HOW TO DEAL WITH SLAVE REVOLTS.
NO ONE BUT HER IS SAYING A THING ABOUT A SLAVE REVOLT, MISTRESS!

WE'RE NOT THE TYPES THAT STAND ON CEREMONY AROUND HERE GUYS.
WE'RE NOT GOING TO SEND YOU PACKING, JUST BECAUSE YOU CAN'T PUT YOUR HANDS ON AN INVITE.
NOT AFTER YOU'VE TRAVELED SUCH A DAMN LONG WAY.
THAT'S REALLY NICE, SIR.
WE REALLY APPRECIATE IT.
YES!
THANK YOU, SIR!
I KNOW WE DIDN'T START OUT ON THE RIGHT FOOTING, BUT WE REALLY ARE NICE PEOPLE!

WELL, YOU CAME TO THE RIGHT PLACE BECAUSE IT'S CANADA. EVERYONE'S NICE HERE.
YOU KNOW I THINK I'VE HEARD THAT!
AND --
I'M ABOUT THE NICEST OF THE FROZEN LOT!
I CAN'T JUST LET YOU WANDER, YOU UNDERSTAND?
NOT YOUR FIRST TIME VISITING US, YOU'D GET LOST FOREVER, AND GOD KNOWS WE WOULDN'T WANT THAT.
AND, YOUNG FELLA, DIDN'T YOU SAY YOU'VE RECENTLY DEVELOPED A THING FOR ASIAN WOMEN.
UH, YEAH!
I HAVE!
OH, NOT THIS AGAIN, MALCOLM!

WELL, I HAVE JUST THE WOMAN FOR YOU, NOW THAT I THINK ABOUT IT.
I'LL JUST CALL DOWN AND HAVE HER COME UP TO MEET YOU.
SHE'LL ACT AS YOUR ESCORT, AND PERHAPS YOU'LL BE LUCKY ENOUGH TO FORM A LOVE CONNECTION.
THAT SOUNDS FANTASTIC!
THANKS A LOT MAN!
AND -- WILL SHE BE ABLE TO TAKE US TO DARCI?
I SHOULDN'T BE SURPRISED.
I'LL JUST GO MAKE THE CALL. YOU GUYS WAIT RIGHT HERE.
CAN YOU BELIEVE IT, MALCOLM --
WE'RE IN!

I'LL END THIS SLAVE REVOLT RIGHT HERE AND NOW!
MISTRESS, WE WERE JUST SUGGESTING THAT EXILE, PERHAPS EVEN TO ELFLAND MIGHT BE THE BETTER OPTION!
THE ELVES REALLY ARE A BUNCH OF NASTY PRICKS, BUT I'M AFRAID YOUR FORMER MISTRESS MIGHT, LIKE NAPOLEON, RETURN SOMEDAY AND TRY TO RECLAIM THIS DOMAIN.
THAT I CAN'T HAVE --
SO --
I'M DUTY BOUND TO HANG HER!
THE MISTRESS MAKES AN EXCELLENT POINT.
I'M SURE WE'D NOT WANT HER BACK EITHER!

FUCK!
COME ON GUYS!
THERE MUST BE A LESS PERMANENT SOLUTION!
LIKE I DON'T MIND BECOMING YOUR PERMANENT SEX BITCH, MISTRESS.
GOD, THIS IS SO MUCH FUN!
I WONDER HOW ALL THIS WOULD GO DOWN WITH MICHAEL?
WHO AM I KIDDING. MICHAEL IS THE ORIGINAL WHEENIE.
HE'D JUST GIVE ME SOME SHIT ABOUT MY CHOICE OF FRIENDS OR SOMETHING.

THE HANGING SCENARIO IS SEXY AND FUN, BUT WHEN DOES ALL THE FUCKING BEGIN?
USING YOU AS MY SEX BITCH HAS ITS POSSIBILITIES, PRETENDER, BUT I BELIEVE THAT ROLE IS ALREADY FILLED --
RIGHT BLONDIE!
Risk Pool
THIS JUST CAN'T BE HAPPENING!
IS THERE A PROBLEM?
Risk Pool
NO MISTRESS, IT'S JUST THAT BEFORE I ARRIVED HERE I THOUGHT I WAS DESTINED FOR GREATER THINGS.
OH, AND WHY WOULDN'T YOU BE?
Risk Pool
IF I DIDN'T SEE POTENTIAL IN YOU WOULD I HAVE ORDERED YOU TO LICK MY SEX, BITCH.
UH?

I DON'T KNOW?
HOW DO YOU THINK I GOT MY START?
Risk Pool
YOU STARTED AS SOMEONE'S SEX BITCH?
AND NOW YOU'RE A FULL-FLEDGED MISTRESS?
IF YOU EMBRACE THE GUILD AS YOUR GUIDING SEXUAL MASTER, YOU CAN BECOME ANYTHING YOU WANT.
ANYTHING, MY THAT DOES SOUND INTRIGUING!
AND -- IF YOU SHOULD CHOOSE TO EMBRACE THE CHARTER INSTEAD, WELL I'M AFRAID YOU MIGHT BE NOTHING MORE THAN A SEX BITCH FOR ALL OF YOUR UNNATURAL SEXUAL EXISTANCE.

IF ALL WE'RE GOING TO DO IS CHAT, I'M HEADING BACK TO FANTASYLAND.
WHAT KIND OF IDIOT RENDERS A DELIGHTFUL MAN'S COCK UTTERLY USELESS?
GRRR!
IT SEEMED LIKE A VIABLE IDEA AT THE TIME.
WHERE WAS I?
THAT DAMN GATOR!
OH, HELL!
DARCI'S COMPLETELY OUT OF HER MIND.
THE SEX BITCH REFERS TO HER AS 'PROFESSOR EVIL', AND PERHAPS SHE'S APTLY NAMED!
I'M ABOUT TO DIE AND SHE'S JUST STANDING THERE MASTURBATING.
IF THAT'S NOT EVIL, THEN WHAT IS?
WELL, WE'LL SEE HOW SHE FEELS WHEN THE NOOSE IS AROUND HER NECK!
THE EVIL ONES ALWAYS GET IT IN THE END!
OH --
WHAT DOES THAT SAY ABOUT ME?

YOU KNOW THE RULES, FRED!
RUMBLE
IF A FLAG IS OUT THERE, SHE'S FIAR GAIME.
ROAR
IF WE MAKE THE CAPTURE, YOU LEAVE THEM ALONE!
RUMBLE
BULLSHIT!
RUMBLE

WHY DO I GET THE FEELING THAT ONE DAY, OLE FRED WILL GO COMPLETELY ROGUE ON US?
I HOPE NOT, LT. THAT WOULD BE ONE BIG UGLY PISSED-OFF GATOR!
OH MY, GOD!
YOU SAVED OUR LIVES!
YEAH, SOMETHING LIKE THAT.
SECURE THE PRISONER!

OH SHIT, I WAS SUPPOSED TO BE RUNNING FROM YOU, WASN'T I?
I'M SORRY, I MESSED UP YOUR TRAINING, BUT --
YOU CAN'T EXPECT ME TO PLAY YOUR GAME WITH A DANGEROUS CREATURE LIKE THAT OUT THERE.
I MEAN SEROUSLY, GUYS!
WE'LL HAVE TO HIDE BRENDA. BRAVO TEAM IS LIKELY NEARBY.
AND -- NO FUCKING AROUND THE MINUTE YOU'RE OUT OF MY SIGHT, SLUT!

NO SEX? COULD THIS SHIT GET ANY WORSE?
OH, QUIT YOUR SNIVELING, FLAG --
JUST BE DAMN GLAD YOU'RE NOT IN DARCI'S COMBAT BOOTS RIGHT NOW.
SO, IS THIS WHERE YOU GUYS BEND ME OVER AN AVAILABLE LOG AND HAVE YOUR WAY WITH ME?
BELIEVE ME, BABY, I'D LOVE TO, BUT THE OLD MAN GET'S PISSED AS HELL IF WE USE A FLAG WITHOUT HIS SAY SO!
THIS IS ALL WAY TOO FUCKED UP, AND IT'S VERY UNLIKE MY USUAL MASTURBATION FANTASIES.
UNFRIENDLY GATORS AND NOT ENOUGH FUCKING!

DAYS
BEFORE
THE EVENT

PLEASE DON'T KILL ME!
JUST TELL ME YOU HAD NOTHING TO DO WITH THIS!
I WAS JUST WASHING MY HANDS.
WHY?
WHY DID THEY DO THAT?
WHY DID THEY ATTACK YOU?
I THINK MY EMPLOYER JUST DELIVERED NOTICE OF MY TERMINATION.
I REALLY SHOULDN'T LEAVE WITNESSES, HONEY.
SHIT, I MUST BE GETTING SOFT.
PLEASE!
TELL THE COPS A 200 LB CAUCASIAN DID THIS, AND I'LL LET YOU LIVE.
THEY'LL LIKELY BELIEVE YOU.
I WILL, AND THANK YOU, MISS.

THANK YOU SO MUCH. I'D LOVE TO NAME MY FIRST CHILD AFTER YOU.
OH WAIT, IF YOU TOLD ME YOURE NAME, YOU'D PROBABLY HAVE TO KILL ME.
MY NAME IS GRACE!
GRACE JENNINGS!
OH, SHIT!
I THINK YOU MIGHT HAVE JUST TALKED YOURSELF OUT OF THE SALE, HONEY!
PLEASE, NOT THE EYE, GRACE. THAT'S JUST GROSS!

THE DOMAINS
SOMETIME DURING THE EVENT

SHIT!
DON'T MAKE A MOVE ELF!
HALF!
WHAT?
I'M A HALF ELF. SEE NO POINTY EARS!
SHOW US YOUR HUNTING PERMIT, ELF.
HALF!
THE REFUSE PROCESSING HALL IS OFF LIMITS TO ALL BUT THOSE WITH A RODENT HUNTING PERMIT.

SO, YOU ARE EITHER A HUNTER OR A RODENT.
WHICH IS IT, SLUT!
LOOK GUYS, I KNOW I SHOULDN'T BE HERE, BUT IT'S SUCH A CONVENIENT CUT THROUGH IF YOU'RE TRAVELING TO ELFLAND.
SO YOU ADMIT IT!
ADMIT WHAT?
THAT YOU'RE AN ELF!
HALF!
AND -- I TRAVEL BACK AND FORTH ALL THE TIME!
WELL, I BELIEVE THIS IS YOUR LAST TRIP, ELF.
HALF!

OOOOH!
HOLY HELL!
WHAT IS THAT SMELL, MISTRESS.
IT'S THE WASTE PROCESSORS BELOW THE CITY.
SO IT'S --
SHIT!

OH, MY GOD, YOU TAKE ME TO THE NICEST PLACES, MISTRESS!
BUT -- I SUPPOSE EVEN SMELLING SHIT IS BETTER THAN A DAGGER IN THE EYE.
ARE YOU EVER GOING TO LET THAT GO, BEAUTIFUL?
PROBABLY NOT!
HOWEVER, I DO --
LOVE BEING YOUR SEX BITCH, MISTRESS!

OH MY GOD, WHAT IS THAT SMELL?
I'LL ADMIT --
IT'S NOT THE MOST FRAGRANT SHORT CUT.
BUT, HERE WE'RE TO MEET YOUR SEXY ASIAN GUIDE SHE'LL TAKE YOU SOMEWHERE MUCH NICER.
FROM WHENCE YOU MORONS WILL NEVER RETURN.
NOT ANOTHER STEP!
THE ELF SLUT IS OURS!
HALF!
OH, HELL!
DANTE!

I'M OFICIALLY LOSING IT!
DANTE!
DANTE!
I'M SORRY, WHAT DID YOU SAY, BABY?
THIS IS YOUR CHANCE TO GET BACK IN THE GAME, GRACE!
YOU PROMISED CANDY, YOU WERE DONE WITH THAT LIFE, GRACE!
THERE'S ONLY ONE REASONABLE APPROACH HERE, GRACE!
OFF THE BITCH AS YOU SHOULD HAVE DONE IN THE FIRST PLACE -- AND MOVE THE FUCK ON!

MOVE AND I'LL PUT ONE IN YOUR EYE!
JESUS!
THAT'S GROSS!
DON'T GET CARRIED AWAY, MISTRESS DIANA!
KILL?
WE HAVE NO INTEREST IN STEALING YOUR KILL. I JUST WANT A WORD WITH MY FRIEND OVER THERE.
JUST LIKE SQUIRRELS, RATS AND PIGEONS, NO ONE EVER ADMITS TO CONSUMING ELVES, BUT I'VE ALWAYS THOUGHT OF THEM AS RATHER GOOD EATING!
HOLY HELL!
COME ALONG, ELF, TIME TO MEET YOUR EVIL MAKER.
COME ON YOU GUYS, HAVE A HEART!
GO TALK TO YOUR FRIEND, DANTE. I'LL JUST KEEP MY EYE ON THESE TWO.

THEY DO SOME REALLY INVOLVED ROLEPLAYING IN THE GROUP.
I'M SO FUCKED!
I'M HAVING A BIT OF A PROBLEM KEEPING UP --
AND, DETERMINING WHERE WE FIT INTO THIS.
I REALLY JUST WANT TO FIND, DARCI.
GRACE, LOSE THE SEX BITCH. WE NEED TO TALK!
GO ON, BABY!
GRRRR!
SEX BITCH, INDEED!
OH, LOOK!
MEN!
YOO HOO!

THEY DON'T MAKE THEM LIKE THAT ANYMORE!
OH, MY!
WOW!
SHE'S THE HUMAN VERSION OF A SEXY FRENCH POODLE.
I'LL BET YOU GUYS SAY THAT TO EVERY NAKED FRENCH POODLEGIRL YOU MEET.
WELL, NOT EVERY-ONE!
ARE YOU SEEING ANYTHING STRANGE, DANTE?
YOU OKAY, GRACE?
NOT REALLY!
YOU LOOK EVEN PALER THAN USUAL!

ANYWAY, SEE THOSE TWO MORONS OVER THERE.
GRRRR!
THE TWO BUSY OGLING MY GIRL?
YES, INDEED, GRACE!
SELLING THIS JOB MIGHT BE MUCH EASIER THAN I FIRST ANTICIPATED.
JOB? WHAT JOB? I'M NOT KILLING ANYONE, DANTE!
YOU, WANT SOMEONE ROUGHED UP -- A BROKEN LEG OR TWO AND I'M YOUR GIRL!
BUT KILLING --
I PROMISED CANDY, I WAS DONE WITH ALL THAT!
C'MON GRACE, IN RETURN FOR THE CHARTER'S SPONSORSHIP AND REFUGE WITHIN THE DOMAINS, YOU AGREED TO DO THE OCCASIONAL ODD JOB FOR US.
BACK IN THE GAME, GRACE --
YOU, KNOW YOU WANT IT!

www.ingramcontent.com/pod-product-compliance
Lightning Source LLC
Chambersburg PA
CBHW082017170626
46817CB00009B/3128
* 9 7 8 1 9 4 8 2 9 7 2 1 9 *